MR. MUSCLE
AND THE STEROIDS SCANDAL

Roger Mee-Senseless

Mr Muscle was the strongest person in all of Mr Man land. He was very proud of this fact.

He enjoyed using his strength to help people, for example: carrying shopping bags for old ladies, helping someone to push start a broken down car, undoing particularly hard to undo bolts etc.

He was nice like that.

He also enjoyed parading around in budgie smugglers.

Not in a pervy way, you understand. You see he was a keen bodybuilder and enjoyed regularly entering competitions.

However, Mr Muscle had a dark secret.

He was a drugs cheat...

Mr Muscle wasn't always the beefcake you see before you. He had always dreamt of being a bodybuilder but despite a healthy diet of meat, fruits and vegetables together with his regular gym workouts he really struggled to put on any bulk.

He was in the gym one day and had lost all motivation.

"What's up?" asked Mr Busybody.

"Problems with your sex life again?"

"How do you know about that?" asked Mr Muscle.

"Little Miss Gobby has told everyone."

"Fucking great," replied Mr Muscle. "No, actually I've got a bodybuilding competition coming up and I need to put on some muscle quick."

"I know someone who can help with that," offered Mr Busybody.

"He's a Russian guy who worked with the Olympic team. He can get you LITERALLY ANYTHING."

"Wow," said Mr Muscle, "that would be amazing."

And so it was that Vitali Kopalotovit became Mr Muscle's strength, conditioning, 'nutrition and lifestyle' coach.

"What we need to do is put you on a programme of full body workouts with isometric and plyometric exercises.

We need to combine this with a strict diet of complex carbs, quality protein, animo acids and a shitload of high strength steroids."

"Whatevs," replied Mr Muscle. "I just wanna get ripped."

Vitali explained his system to Mr Muscle and put him straight onto his intensive course of steroids. He took so many pills that if you had shaken him he would've sounded like a maraca.

And he had so many injections of who knows what that his arse looked like a pin cushion.

Mr Muscle soon noticed that he was quickly becoming stronger and that he was beating his personal bests in each and every lifting discipline.

He did notice some side effects though - his penis and balls were starting to shrivel up at an alarming rate and he was experiencing some pretty intense mood swings.

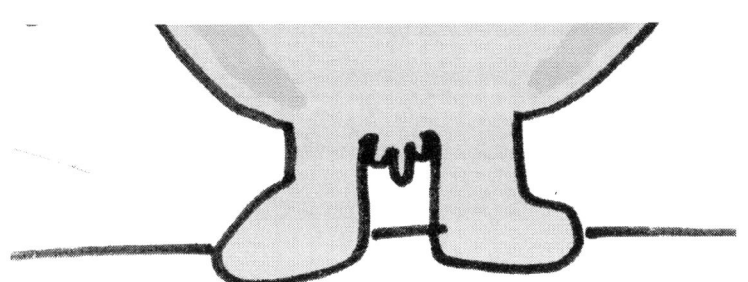

Vitali assured him that all of this was normal and would be 'totally worth it'. He went on the explain that if Mr Muscle followed his advice to the letter there was no chance that the doping tests would detect even a trace of an illegal substance.

"And if the worst happens then we'll just ask Mr Nice to piss in a cup for you and we'll be golden," he said cheerily.

DIRECT SPORTS

up to

120% OFF EVERYTHING

We'll pay you to take it.

obviously we won't

BUY ONE SHOE FOR TWICE THE USUAL PRICE AND GET THE OTHER HALF PRICE

Mr Muscle trusted Vitali and continued to make good progress. He handled the side effects and really began to believe he could achieve his dream of being a national, or even international, bodybuilding champion.

He was well used to being one of the strongest men in Mr Man Land but, as Mr Sweary quite rightly said, "Mr Man Land is fully of absolute pussyholes."

After several more months training Vitali told Mr Muscle that he was competition ready. "The last thing that you need is some gravy browning to give you a nice deep tan to show off your definition and the smallest, and I mean smallest pair of speedos you can get a hold of to show of your tiny cock and balls," he instructed.

Mr Muscle got quite angry at that point, and then began to cry.

The competition was only days away but Mr Muscle then hit a rather large problem. Vitali had disappeared.

Mr Muscle tried to call him but the number wouldn't connect. He began to worry. He suspected that he had probably been picked up by the authorities. If he was lucky it would be by the police and if he was unlucky, the KGB.

Mr Muscle resigned himself to the fact that he was probably not going to see him again.

Little did he know that, inexplicably, Vitali had simply jetted off to Benidorm on a last minute holiday.

Mr Muscle became concerned that the drugs in his system were maybe not as untraceable as Vitali had claimed. It was a little difficult to pinpoint why he felt like this but one of the reasons was that his piss was bright blue and was fizzier than a can of pop that you'd just shaken up.

So it would appear that he would need Mr Nice's help after all. He tracked him down and explained the plan to him, which would need him to stand outside the toilet window around the back of the bodybuilding venue to drop off a wee sample, at a pre determined time, that Mr Muscle could pass off as his own.

Before that Mr Strong had some shopping to attend to. Vitali had left him a short shopping list...

TINY speedos
(for parading around in)

Gravy browning
(as much as you can get -
to give you a deep tan)

A chicken and mushroom
Pot Noodle
(just cus I fancy one)

So the first stop was the swimwear section of his local 'Direct Sports' shop who, as luck would have it, were having an 'up to 80% off sale' that very day.

"Jesus Christ that's good luck," Mr Muscle said to no-one in particular.

He quickly tracked down some nice looking bright blue speedos with red stripes down the side. The only problem was that they just weren't tight enough, even the extra small size.

Mr Muscle decided to go and have a look in the children's section. He picked up a similar pair of speedos that were labelled 11 to 12 years old in one hand and a pair labelled 8 to 9 in his other hand. Unsure which ones he'd be able to get on and not have to be cut out of he pondered for a moment.

5 later and the police arrived to question the 'strange looking 20 stone man attempting to try on an infant's pair of budgie smugglers in the middle of the shop floor.

a family of budgies

Fortunately the police believed his defence that he was 'just a bit of a twat' and he left the store with his purchase tucked in his shirt pocket.

Keen to make up time after the whole police mix up Mr Muscle raced to Sainsco to pick up the gravy browning.

He asked the assistant, Mr Jumble, where the gravy was.

"We don't have any of that," said Mr Jumble.

"Shiiiiit, are you sure? said a disappointed Mr Muscle, who felt himself tearing up again.

"No, we definitely don't have any of that."

"Actually, isn't that it there?" replied Mr Muscle.

"Oh yes, sorry, I was thinking of custard," said Mr Jumble.

"Twat," said Mr Muscle.

Gravy browning
Not Gravy browning
SAINSCO
VALUE
Gravy
Browning
THICK
CUSTARD

Hoping there would be enough, he cleared the shelf of the 10 available bottles, paid for them and rushed out of the shop.

On the way home he passed Mr Jumble who had realised that today was actually his day off. He was also going the wrong way.

What an absolute fucking tool, thought Mr Muscle.

As soon as he was home he chucked the contents of the bottles into the bath and jumped in.

He covered himself from head to foot, and all of the crooks and crannies in between then stood, dripping, in front of the mirror to practice grimacing.

"I look AMAZING," he said to his reflection, modestly.

He arrived at the competition in good time, so he had a look around and sized up the competition.

Mr Muscle felt confident. He went to the changing rooms and put on his tiny, child size speedos and gave himself a final once over.

A couple of the other competitors, who Mr Muscle thought must be rank amateurs had waited until the last moment to apply their gravy browning.

Maybe they have cream leather seats in their cars and didn't want to stain it, who knows.

One of them asked Mr Muscle to help out. Thinking tactically Mr Muscle said casually, "Yeh, no problem, always happy to help out another strongman."

He then let out a little evil laugh, which he hoped wasn't audible as he drew a cock and balls onto the man's back.

MUHAHA
HAHHA
HAHHA
HAH

Well that's one less person in the running, he thought to himself as he accepted the man's thank yous.

Mr Muscle spied another competitor stood against the wall being carefully sprayed with Cuprinol creosote.

Apparently he'd got the idea from reading David Dickinson's autobiography, 'Dickinson: Made from teak'.

Mr Muscle casually walked past the spray machine and accidentally nudged it to 'ultra high pressure'.

One of Mr Muscle's other dirty tricks was to call the venue from his phone and tell them that one of the other competitors had a family emergency to attend to.

He watched in amusement as they ran out of the hall in a panic and then imagined their face as they received the 'emergency message' asking them what flavour Findus crispy pancakes they wanted for tea.

It was soon time to stride out onto the stage to line up against the other competitors. It was quite a big X Factor/Britain's Got Talent/Insert other shit generic talent show here, affair with a panel of judges casting their beady eyes upon them.

Vitali had told him that the best way to tense up your muscles for maximum effect is to imagine you're having a massive shit that just won't come out. That way your entire body ripples and your face looks extra tight.

He put all of this into practice and as the judges began to announce the winners in reverse order, Mr Strong grew more and more tense.

Finally, after they had announced all of the trophy winners they called, "And the grand winner of this year's Bodybuilding championships is.... MR STRONG!"

He was absolutely delighted and graciously ran around the room with the trophy making loser signs at everyone.

Mr Strong basked in the glory for days and enjoyed the attention the title brought him, especially from the 'ladiessssss'.

However it was short lived, he received a serious sounding message from the strongman committee. He called them back immediately.

"Mr Strong. I'm afraid that there has been a problem. The urine sample that you provided has tested positive for 17 different banned substances.

"There must be some problem!" said Mr Strong. "This can't be right."

"We ran the tests 4 times because we couldn't believe it ourselves. The doctor said that he's surprised that you're not dead."

Mr Strong wracked him brains, what could possibly have happened? He was sure that he'd covered all bases.

He decided to go and see Mr Nice. He knocked on the door and waited. And waited. And waited.

There was no sign of life. Mr Nice's neighbour was Mr Busybody, who came out to see what was going on.

"I haven't seen him for 6 and a half hours, which is strange because he usually goes to buy the paper between 11.05 and 11.15," said Mr Busybody.

Mr Strong decided to kick the door down. Taking a few steps backwards he charged towards the door and threw all of his hefty weight into it. The door splintered like a rotten twig and Mr Strong ended up in a heap on the floor.

Mr Busybody, who Mr Strong thought looked suitably impressed, stood over him and said, "You could've just used my spare key but never mind."

Together they searched the house for Mr Nice. They found him in the bath, stone dead.

It turned out that Mr Nice was hooked on all manner of street drugs. You see he lived in a fairly rough part of town and every time a dealer offered him drugs he was too nice to turn them down.

wanna buy some drugs?
I've got
smack
toot
blow
crystal
moon rocks
nitrous
looney toons
fizzies
yes please, that would be lovely

This led to Mr Strong being stripped of his title. He didn't have a leg to stand on. Even if he came clean no one would believe his story about Mr Nice anyway.

He stopped taking the steroids on the spot. His body went into shock and he died of a huge heart attack.

Vitali had a great time in Benidorm and came back with a massive toblerone.

12980244R00023